PEOPLE, PEOPLE, EVERYWHERE!

by Nancy Van Laan

illustrated by Nadine Bernard Westcott

Alfred A. Knopf · New York

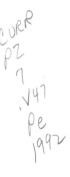
THIS IS A BORZOI BOOK
PUBLISHED BY ALFRED A. KNOPF, INC.

Library of Congress Cataloging-in-Publication Data

Van Laan, Nancy.
  People, people, everywhere! / by Nancy Van Laan ; illustrated by
Nadine Bernard Westcott.
    p.   cm.
  Summary: Describes the effects of the nation's population growth
in rhymed text and illustrations.
    ISBN 0-679-81063-3 (trade) — ISBN 0-679-91063-8 (lib. bdg.)
    [1. Population—Fiction.   2. Humorous stories.   3. Stories in
rhyme.]   I. Westcott, Nadine Bernard, ill.   II. Title.
PZ8.3.V34Pe   1992
[E]—dc20   90-5303

Manufactured in Singapore
10 9 8 7 6 5 4 3 2 1

For Anne Schwartz, a splendid editor and friend
—N. V. L.

To Sarah and Bobby S.
—N. B. W.

People, people, everywhere!
Running here, running there!
People racing round the town,
Going up!
Going down!
People riding to the top.
Getting off!
Please press *STOP!*

People dashing round the park,
Walking dogs…
Bark! Bark! Bark!

People waiting in a line.
Here's the bus!
Just in time!

Catching taxis…catching trains…
Catching subways…catching planes.
Take a copter
Up! Up! Up!
Take a ferry,
Shlup! Shlup! Shlup!

People, people, everywhere!
Working here, working there.
Policemen walking city beats.
Vendors selling treats to eat.

Workers building buildings tall,
Way up high.
Watch out! Don't fall!

People working under town,
Digging, fixing, underground.
Tunneling subways, sealing leaks,
Way beneath the city streets.

CLOSED FOR REPAIRS

Teachers teaching...plumbers plumbing...
Doctors doctoring...drummers drumming...

Here's a fire truck
Whizzing, wailing!
In the harbor,
Boats are sailing!

Children, children, everywhere!
Playing here, playing there.
In the alleys…at the park…
In the hallways after dark.
Jumping rope, playing ball,
Playing anything at all!
Riding bikes, tic-tac-toe,
Children shouting, "Go! Go! Go!"
Upstairs, downstairs,
Running round,
Children playing all through town!

People, people, everywhere!
Leaving here, going there.
Moving to a quiet place
In the country where there's space.
Room to work and room to play,
No more waiting every day.

No more traffic, no more noise,
Lots of space for lots of toys.
Trees and flowers all around,

A perfect place to build a town.

For Sale

For Sale

For Sale

Sold

For Sale

For Sale

FOR SALE

People here, people there,

People, people, everywhere!

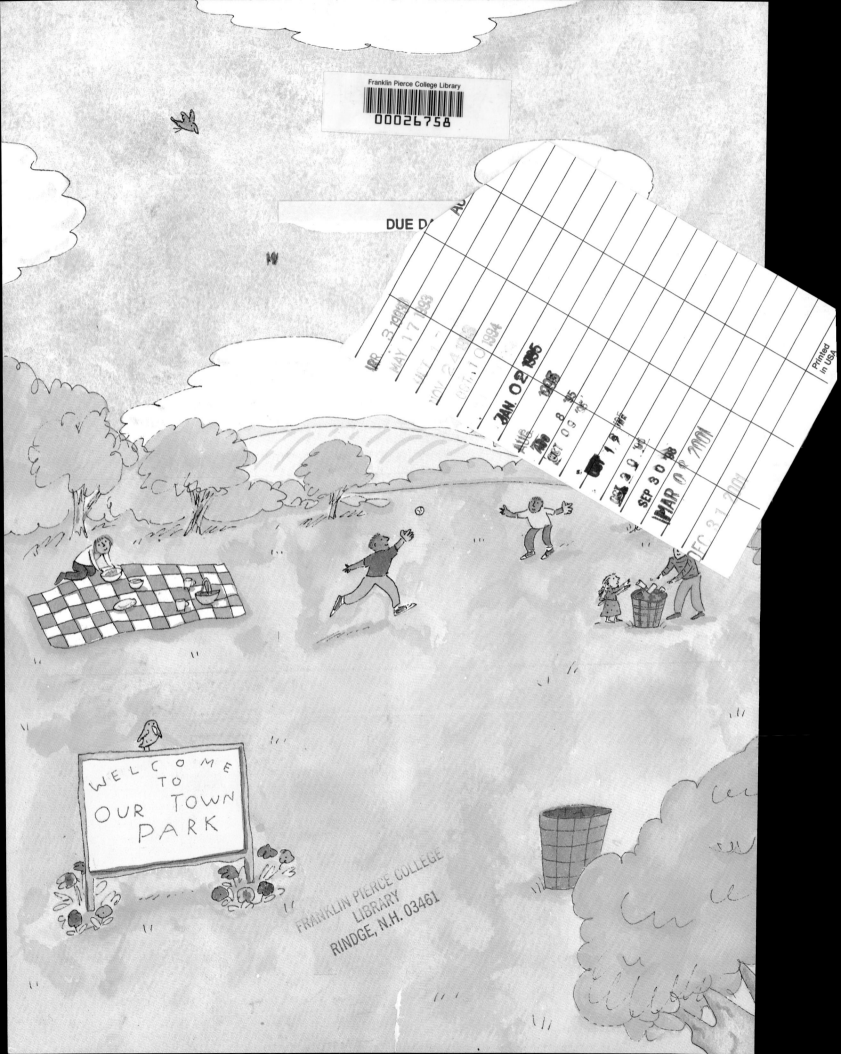